FROM ERIK'S DIARY
(LORELAI AND I)

EPISODE 4

A STRANGE
DIMENSION

Massimo Indrio

© Massimo Indrio
www.massimoindrio.com
first edition: November 2014
ISBN: 978-88-940304-3-3
Translation by Brett Auerbach-Lynn

CHAPTER 1

People are strange, the world is strange, life is strange. The more you dwell on thoughts of this sort the more everything starts to seem absurd. Though in the end, when it really comes down to it, there's really nothing strange about it. It's just the way things are.

These were the profound philosophical concepts I was mulling over, lazily lounging on the purple checkered armchair in the blue parlor and looking out through the colored window panes at the people passing by on the street when, with a feline leap, Lorelai jumped into my arms and announced, "I'm pregnant!"

These two brief but unmistakable words passed through my ears, went down the narrow spiral staircase of my subconscious, and pried open a door which until then had been sealed shut. My mind's eye was thus presented with a series of fleeting prophetic visions. First I saw a newborn baby being affectionately tended to by a caring mother. But as the boy grew older, he had to suffer through a rigid Spartan education that slowly transformed him into the man of strong and resolute character who

would take over the world, ruining it completely. I was already searching for a solution to
avoid this deplorable sequence of events when
Lorelai's silvery laugh brought me back down
to earth.

"Don't worry, my credulous little sweetie
pie," she said, kissing me, "it's not true at all. I
was just joking. But look, a letter came for me
today from the Principality of Minutia."

And so it was that once more, Lorelai quite
brusquely brought me down from the rarified
air of my abstract contemplations to the fla-
tlands of practical and contingent matters which, at least in her case, were often even more
abstract – or better, abstruse – than my own
meditations.

"Are you in the mood for joking around today?" I asked her, taking from her hands a large yellow envelope covered in coats of arms,
stamps, and wax seals.

It came in fact from the Principality of Minutia, a state which I had never heard of. The envelope was already open so I pulled out the
letter, this too written on yellow paper, and
read: "Dear Madame or Mademoiselle. Since
you have sent us five-hundred bottle caps of
Zam Unripe Cucumber Juice, we are pleased to
inform you that you have won First Prize in the
Zam contest, consisting in the title of Princess
of Minutia with all of its appurtenances. Your
Lordship is expected for the investiture ceremony on the evening of the 23rd day of the cur-

rent month. On that very same morning General Felix Cannon will come to escort you. Congratulations and regards, Prime Minister Astrogogolo."

"Astrogogolo? Felix Cannon?" I said, putting down the letter. "Just what kind of names do they have in that place?"

"Is that really what most surprises you?" Lorelai asked, staring at me with her big blue eyes open wide.

"No. What most surprises me is that you and I alone drank five-hundred bottles of unripe cucumber juice. Don't you think we might have overdone it just a little?"

"Well maybe, but it's so tasty …"

"I'm curious to see just where this Principality of Minutia is!" I exclaimed, jumping to my feet and setting off towards the library at the top of the tower. Lorelai followed.

Here was my chance to test out the purchase I'd made the previous month in the Grand Bazaar in Istanbul, where in the course of a clandestine auction I'd succeeded in knocking down the sphere of the sorceress Onofria. It was a transparent opal the size of a soccer ball that always provided exact answers to any questions it was asked. I would have liked to have tried it out at the moment of purchase, but a surprise police raid on the secret auction's premises rapidly dispersed all the participants, me included. To avoid capture I took refuge in a nearby opium bar, where the air was so thick with smoke that merely breathing it in was enough to find myself floating in a pink sky and chasing after little golden ducks that were hopping from one little cloud to another. Fortunately no one took advantage of my momentary stupor to steal my magic sphere, probably because they were all even more dazed than I was.

In any case the time had come to finally test it out, especially since I now had the instructions as well. I removed the sphere from its black velvet bag and the sheet of instructions fell to the ground. I picked it up and discovered to my chagrin that it was written in Arabic. Luckily, being a polyglot was one of Lorelai's innumerable qualities so I passed it over to her.

After taking a quick look at it she told me, "It's very simple. You just knock three times on the crystal ball and then formulate your question."

I immediately did as she'd told me and asked just where the Principality of Minutia was located. A few seconds passed in which nothing at all happened, and then out of nowhere I received a resounding slap in the face from an invisible hand.

Lorelai carefully examined the red mark stamped on my cheek and observed, "It seems like woman's hand. Maybe it was the sorceress Onofria."

"Yeah, but what I would like to know is why," I replied, massaging my aching cheek.

"Who knows ... try repeating the question."

"Not a chance. One slap in the face is more than enough for me. Is there anything else written in the instructions?"

Lorelai reopened the piece of paper, examined it more carefully, and then exclaimed, "Well I'll be, I didn't see this. Underneath it's written that good manners are very important and thus every question must be phrased using the word 'please,' or else the just punishment will unfailingly arrive."

"Unfailingly, is it?"

"Oh yeah, that's exactly what it says."

Precision was unfortunately *not* one of Lorelai's innumerable qualities.

"Are you sure it doesn't say anything else?" I asked, just to be sure.

"Oh no, there's nothing else. You can be sure of that."

So I knocked once again on the sphere and repeated my question without forgetting this time to say the magic word. It suddenly lit up with a tenuous glow, and letters - no, they were numbers - appeared. It didn't take me long to figure out that they indicated geographic coordinates. I took down the numbers and, before doing anything else, thanked the sphere very politely so as to avoid other unforeseen punishments.

Locating that point took no time at all since I kept maps of almost the whole world in a basket right there in the library. I'd drawn them myself in my time as cartographer for Professor Von Stratosferik.

There was a surprise in store for us, however. We were quite amazed indeed to discover that those coordinates indicated the latitude and longitude of our very own city.

CHAPTER 2

"This crystal ball doesn't work!" I exclaimed. "There are only two possible explanations: either I was conned at that auction, or the sorceress Onofria was a moron."

I immediately realized my mistake, but it was too late. Out of nowhere I was on the receiving end of another slap twice as hard as the first one, and seeing as I was on my feet, I only just avoided losing my balance and ending up on the ground.

Lorelai rushed to console me. Caressing me and kissing the cheek in question, she said to me, "My inconsiderate little sweetie pie, you really shouldn't be so rash. You'll see there's bound to be another explanation."

She was right. My conclusions had been too hasty. Maybe there really was another explanation that for the moment had escaped me. The only other hypothesis that came to mind was that the Principality of Minutia didn't exist at all and this whole story was only a stupid joke.

This time however I kept my conjectures to myself and said simply, "I'd say we forget about it for the moment and get on with our lives. The 23rd is tomorrow, so if General Bazooka comes to pick you up tomorrow morning we'll ask him for an explanation."

"Cannon," said Lorelai.

"What?"

"The general's name is Cannon, not Bazooka."

"Right. In any case we'll ask him for information."

For dinner we made ourselves a Habsburg pepper pizza, really wonderful, and then went to hear a concert for violin, tuba, and fife being held outdoors in the park next to the pagoda. I personally could have done without, but Lorelai insisted because there were musicians from the northern countries where she was born and it was important to her that I hear the music of her native land.

Although I was a bit jaded, the concert ended up being quite enjoyable. The music was beautiful, joyous, and at times even funny. I realized that these three adjectives also fit Lorelai quite well and asked myself if everyone was like this, up there where she was from. By the end of the concert I'd completely forgotten about the letter and the Principality of Minutia, but as we were crossing the park on our way home, a thin bald man with a long thin black moustache wrapped up in black cloak popped out from behind a tree and, after coming closer, whispered to us threateningly: "You poor deluded fools, the throne of Minutia cannot be bought with some ridiculous bottle caps." Then he yelled "Long live Princess Giovanna!", pulled out a long dagger, and raised it to strike Lorelai.

With a quick move of jin-ku-fritz I disarmed him, spun him around, and gave him a kick that sent him scampering away, though I almost immediately regretted this last move since it allowed him to escape. Indeed, in a few moments that scoundrel disappeared entirely into the dark of night. I ought to have treated him to the disorienting triple slap my great master Pun-Jin-Ball had always advised me to use at such times, but now it was too late for recriminations.

Fortunately Lorelai hadn't been frightened at all, perhaps because everything had happened so quickly that she hadn't even had time to realize what was going on. In fact she asked me, "What did that guy want to sell you?"

As if I were in the habit of treating street vendors that way!

So as not to alarm her I replied, "A kitchen knife, didn't you see?"

"No, I was absorbed in my thoughts."

"What were you thinking about?"

"If only you knew, sweetie pie. Tonight's music took me back to the time when as a child my friend Roxanna and I amused ourselves by pushing snow off the roof onto the heads of the people walking down below."

"A wonderful pastime."

"Yeah, it was a lot of fun, at least until Roxanna herself fell down below. She wasn't hurt, but our little operation was discovered. There was a scandal and my father, who was mayor at the time, had to step down. Even my mother who was a seamstress had to close her shop and my dog Oscar had to close his doghouse."

I looked at her with one eyebrow raised and she said, smiling, "Just kidding, Oscar did no such thing."

I still wasn't completely sure that she hadn't been aware of the recent assault. Perhaps while I was pretending nothing was wrong she was doing the same, but even more so. In any case one thing was certain: if she really did have to go to the Principality of Minutia, then I was going with her.   When we got home Lorelai went straight to bed, but I stayed up reading the third volume of Musdosky's horror stories in the green study. Since I'm not afraid of anything, I often read such things in order to get sleepy before going to bed.

That evening I happened onto a particularly engrossing story, whose main character, a certain Mary, after being locked in a tower for three years and despairing all that time, finally discovered that the door to her cell had never been closed. When she came downstairs she found her husband, Count George, hard at work whipping himself up some French fries, he asked her, "Mind telling me what you've been doing up there in the tower?"

Not knowing what to respond, Mary was quite embarrassed and resolved to go back up. But she found her old cell locked shut with a 'Do Not Disturb' sign hung on the door.

Absorbed as I was in the story, I'd lost track of time despite the fact that the gloomy tolls of the great oak pendulum clock marked each hour with the utmost precision. A slight rustling at my back alerted me to the presence of something or someone who, rather than comfortably minding his p's and q's in his own home, had had the bright idea of coming over uninvited to pay me a visit at this ungodly hour. I turned around and found before me what seemed to be at first glance and then revealed himself truly to be, undoubtedly and unmistakably him, none other than Death.

CHAPTER 3

There was no mistaking him. Who else could that skeleton wrapped up from head to toe in a black cloak with a long sickle in hand be? If it was only a costume, it was certainly the best one I'd ever seen.

I was about to turn into the hairy, sharp-toothed monster, Grunz, as I always did whenever I felt threatened when Death, who was clearly well-acquainted with me, said, "Grunz, down boy." As soon as he spoke I knew right off that this was no charade; for his voice was high and low, near and far, clear and unclear all at the same time. I also realized that this time the monster Grunz wouldn't be much help so I blocked the oncoming transformation.

Death asked me, "Aren't you going to invite me to sit down?"

Since he was being so informal, I did the same and said, "Please, have a seat."

He opted for the yellow armchair, which was not a wise choice since it was extremely soft, being stuffed with gauzy sheep's wool, and Death, thin as a skeleton, sank in up to his neck. I helped him back up and escorted him to a small, wood-carved chair I'd picked up in Africa that was more suitable.

"You'll be wondering why I've come to see you," he said to me once he'd made himself comfortable.

"Should I be wondering?"

I found his visit very annoying and inopportune and had no intention of giving him any satisfaction.

"I certainly think so."

"Well I think not. But if you really want to tell me, get on with it because it's late and I want to go to bed."

There was a moment of silence. Perhaps Death wasn't expecting such a cool welcome on my part. Finally he decided to lay his cards on the table, saying dryly, "Your hour has come. You must come with me."

"I'd come most willingly," I responded, "but unfortunately right now I just can't."

"You have no choice," replied my exceedingly boney guest.

"You see," I explained to him, "tomorrow I'll most likely have to accompany my girlfriend to the Principality of Minutia. You won't believe it but they want to crown her princess. Yes, I know, it seems absurd, but it's the honest truth. I fear that there might be complications, and that's why I have to go with her."

"I don't think you understand," Death insisted. "You must cease making plans because your time is up."

"I'm sorry but I have to disagree with you. While everything might point towards you're being right, that's simply not the case. You really should've recognized the chair you're sitting on. It belonged to the witchdoctor Urubu of the Turutuku tribe, who infused it with a potent spell to prepare for your visit to take away his favorite wife. As by now you'll certainly have remembered, because of this spell you were forced to make a deal with him and play him at marbles for his wife."

"Yes, I remember it well, but in the end I won."

"That's true, but the game lasted a long time. A tournament of one hundred and twenty rounds that continued for over thirty years."

"I see that you are very well-informed. Did you happen to be expecting my visit?"

"Absolutely not. It's pure chance that that chair was here close at hand. The witchdoctor Urubu gave it to me as a gift after concealing it in the trunk of my jeep so as to save it from the attack of his eighteen furious wives who'd discovered he'd been cheating on them."

At that moment Lorelai appeared at the door in her nightgown, her eyes sleepy and a glass of water in her hand.

"What are you doing, my nocturnal sweetie pie, aren't you coming to bed?" she asked.

"I'll be there in five minutes," I replied.

As she went back to bed, she added, "How

strange, it seemed like you were talking to an empty seat."

Once we were alone again, Death asked me, "So what do you propose to do? Do you too want to play marbles?"

"No, no marbles. My favorite game is chess, and since I don't like things to drag on for too long a single game will be sufficient. Like in that film with the knight who played chess with Death, remember? I think it was called "The Seventh Wheel" or something like that. It wasn't bad, apart from the ending."

"That depends on your point of view. I saw it as well and quite liked the ending."

"I don't doubt it. Nearly everyone died."

"There's no accounting for taste."

"This is also true. So is chess all right with you?"

"Fine, we shall begin tomorrow."

That said, Death disappeared and for a moment I continued staring into space without thinking about anything. Then I placed the book I'd been reading on the table, got up from the armchair, stretched, and went to bed.

CHAPTER 4

After being up late the previous night I would have loved to sleep a bit later than usual, but at dawn a loud ringing of the doorbell at the front entrance rudely awakened both Lorelai and me. I put on my flowery white nightgown and went to answer the door while Lorelai rolled over with every intention of going back to sleep. Frankly I'm not fond of either nightgowns or slippers because I consider them a bit debauched, but that showy dressing gown had been a birthday gift from Lorelai and I couldn't *not* wear it, at least occasionally. As for the penguin-shaped slippers, I'd immediately said I wouldn't wear them, so I went to open the door in my dressing gown and boots.

I pulled the lever connected to the chain that raised the bar that locked the front door down below, and leaned over from the vast stone landing to see the nutcase who'd gotten it into his head to drag us out of bed at that pre-dawn hour.

The man who entered really did appear to have a screw loose. He wore a military uniform that recalled those of the Napoleonic army, but even more those pompous liveries that doormen at fancy hotels used to wear in the early twentieth century.

No longer young but still in good shape, he had a long gray moustache that connected with his sideburns to form quite a nice pair of side-whiskers. As soon as he came into the large courtyard he stood at attention, brought a trumpet to his lips, and began blowing into it with all the breath his body could muster.

I have never had a great love for that instrument, especially in a military context. I really can't stand blaring trumpet wake-up calls because they remind me of a not particularly happy period when, not yet knowing I was allergic to military discipline, I had hastily enrolled in the Foreign Legion.

On the landing was a wooden tub I'd put out to catch the rain water that dripped down from a point where the roof tiles had been dislodged. It was supposed to be a temporary solution, but since I'd put off the repair work for so long the basin was now almost completely full. It's clearly preferable never to be this impulsive, but the monster Grunz that was always dozing inside me interpreted the presence of that stranger who'd come at dawn to sound the trumpet in our home as an out-and-out attack, not serious enough to produce the normal transformation but still sufficient to unleash an adequate reaction.

A few moments later that poor unknown soldier – in the sense that I didn't know him – found himself soaked to the bone and was forced to bring his trumpet solo to a grinding halt. He'd nonetheless achieved his goal since he'd succeeded in waking Lorelai as well, who joined me on the landing in her nightgown.

"What's going on?" she asked. "Who is that man who is all soaking-wet? Is he in the marching band?"

As soon as the soldier saw Lorelai, he first shook off some of the water as a dog might, and then rushed up the stairs. Mistaking his intentions I blocked his way, but he rounded me quite ably and went to kneel at her feet.

"Princess," he said, "I bring you my greetings. I am General Felix Cannon and I'm here to escort you to the Principality of Minutia for your coronation."

"Oh!" Lorelai exclaimed. "And how come you're all wet? Is it raining?"

"This individual," he said, glaring at me, "whom I suspect to be a Minutian rebel, tried to stop me with a water bomb. Now if you'll excuse me, I'll run him through."

He rose to his feet and pulled out his sword but Lorelai stopped him.

"Wait!" she cried out. "It's all a misunderstanding. He's not a Minutian rebel, he's my boyfriend."

My 'boyfriend'? What a strange way to describe me. I'm certainly not old, but neither am

I a boy. I then remembered that the previous evening I too had said 'my girlfriend' while talking about her with Death, so I concluded that there really wasn't anything that strange about her referring to me like this.

"He might not be a Minutian, but he certainly is a rebel!" exclaimed General Cannon as he sheathed his sword. In truth he was more right than he knew. I'd always had the soul of a rebel, especially when it came to the obtuseness of certain types of people.

"My dear general," I said to him, "I apologize for your unexpected shower but I suggest that next time, before you begin sounding the muster or the charge or the wake-up call or whatever it is, you be more conscious of where you are and what time it is. You see, not all the world is a barracks and above all, a princess cannot be woken up in the same way as a soldier. If you'd played the transverse flute or the bass viol instead of the trumpet, I assure you that no one would have had any cause for complaint."

He glared at me again, then huffed and finally turned to Lorelai, saying, "And now princess, if you'll just follow me we can depart."

"You don't honestly think I'm going to come dressed like this, in my nightgown! Come in for a moment and dry off while we get ready for the trip."

"What do you mean, 'we'? You're not bringing *him* along?"

"If you want her," I cut him short, "you'll have to take me as well."

Then I took Lorelai by the arm and together we went to make our preparations. After two more huffs, General Cannon followed us muttering under his breath.

CHAPTER 5

When we were ready, we went to get the general who was waiting for us in the laundry room where he'd dried out his clothes with the aid of a couple of portable heaters and a hair-dryer. When we got there he'd just put his clothes back on, so we were now ready to raise the anchor.

Before, while we were getting dressed and having breakfast, we'd amused ourselves imagining the means of transport by which General Cannon would escort us to the Principality of Minutia. I'd guessed a black limousine while Lorelai had dreamt up a carriage drawn by white horses, à la Cinderella. The reality however was very different. We discovered, parked in front of our door, an old, high-powered motorcycle complete with sidecar. It was undoubtedly a fine looking object, though perhaps not particularly suitable considering the circumstances.

The general had also strangely changed his attitude toward me. He was now very polite and it made me suspicious. I started to climb into the back seat, thus leaving the sidecar for Lorelai, but he insisted on doing the contrary. I agreed but there was a problem. I couldn't get my legs in because a large bag in the back part of the sidecar was in the way.

"Excuse me, general," I said, "but your bag is in my way. We'll have to put it somewhere else."

"But I don't have a bag," affirmed the whiskered soldier, after which he showed surprising agility in performing a rapid somersault, grabbing the bag by the handles and flinging it high in the air towards the park. At the highest point of its trajectory the bag exploded into a thousand pieces and all of us ended up flat on our backs. Luckily no one was hurt. The only passerby present at that moment was old Count Archibugio de' Cocchi, deaf as a doorpost, who turned to us and asked, "What did you say? Did you call me?"

We got to our feet. As I dusted myself off I said to General Cannon, "Evidently not everyone approves of this investiture. Do you have any idea who might have placed the bomb?"

"Bomb?" he replied scornfully. "You call that big firecracker a bomb? It's obvious that you've never seen a real one. During the war against the dragon-men, in 3012, there were bombs that did more than merely tousle your hair, I guarantee you!"

Dragon-men? 3012? Lorelai and I looked at each other, and in our eyes you could read the

same questions: was General Cannon completely mad? Was it really prudent to go with him?
Had we turned off the gas before going out?
But we had no intention of renouncing this little
adventure so we said nothing and got settled
in our seats, at which point the general started
the engine, then yelled: "Troops of my tripe,
hold on tight!" and finally we were off.

This last sortie of his didn't appear very normal to me either, but again I decided not to
comment. The motorcycle was making a hell of
a racket, as if rather than gas in the tank there
was a mix of whisky, turpentine, and beans.
But it sure flew like a rocket. Fortunately at
that hour the roads were almost completely
empty.

As soon as we departed, it occurred to me
that, contrary to what I had planned, I hadn't
yet asked the general where the Principality of
Minutia was located. I tried asking him now but
there was too much noise and despite yelling
as loudly as I could, I couldn't make myself
heard. Or perhaps he was just pretending not
to hear me. Anyway we were getting further
and further away from our city, so it was clear
that Minutia didn't have the same geographic
coordinates as Onofria's sphere had indicated.
I was once again regretting being victimized in
that scam auction in Istanbul when I realized
that, after taking a quick spin through the
countryside, we were once again heading toward the city. This time I was more determined

than ever to get an explanation from General Cannon, but he didn't give me the time. He pulled a small lever and the sidecar detached from the motorcycle, going off the road and continuing its course through the fields.

After bouncing around in the dirt for a bit, my rickety little wagon finally came to a halt. I got out and watched from afar as the motorcycle went back into the city without me. I was already beginning to transform into the hairy, sharp-toothed monster, Grunz, to catch up with them in three or four leaps, when all of a sudden I saw Lorelai, the general and the motorcycle disappear in a flash of light.

I'd never seen anything like it. What had happened? Where the devil had they gone? What could I do to get them back? Or better still, what could I do to get Lorelai back? For in all sincerity, I couldn't have cared less about General Cannon. I analyzed the situation. Lorelai had disappeared and I found myself in the middle of a field at an hour in which I was usually just beginning – maybe – to open my eyes, still undecided whether to abandon the realm of Morpheus or postpone everything for another half-hour. In any case going back to sleep was out of the question. Now was the moment to act, but I still didn't know what to do. As I stood there scratching my head, a little bird landed on the branch of an olive tree right beside me. It looked at me for several moments, moving its head right and then left, and then began to chirp. I thought it might have a suggestion for me but, unfortunately, I couldn't understand what it was saying.

The sun had now been up for some time and with the light there were also more cars on the road. I set off on foot towards the city, trying to hitch a ride along the way. Unexpectedly, a small truck carrying fruit stopped. The driver was a jovial fellow who loved telling jokes, but as much as I forced myself to play along, I was in no mood for laughter.

CHAPTER 6

I got home and sank into the red armchair in the orange living room and immediately started racking my brains for a plan of action. In the past that red armchair had shown itself on other occasions to be the most suitable place for quick and profitable thinking. It lived up to its reputation this time as well. A few minutes sufficed to come up with the right idea. In the end all you had to do was properly analyze the facts and draw the proper conclusions.

The motorcycle had been heading back towards town. This could have been a confirmation of what Onofria's sphere had said the night before, that the geographic coordinates of Minutia and our city were one and the same. If the sphere was not spouting nonsense, then the best thing to do was go question it further.

Whether or not it was due to the red armchair, I had quickly come to a satisfying conclusion, but as I was getting up to run to the library I felt a chill down run my spine and saw Death appear in front of me with a chessboard under his arm.

"Here I am," he said, placing the chessboard on the table and sitting down in front of me. "Are you ready to begin our game?"

"I'm terribly sorry but right now I really can't," I hastily replied, and then as I ran out of the room, I added, "We have the whole day ahead of us, let's wait until later."

Once I'd reached the library, I once more pulled the sphere out of its velvet bag, knocked on it three times, and asked, "Can you please tell me where Lorelai is?"

The words appeared suspended in the usual tenuous glow: "In the Principality of Minutia."

"I suspected as much," I thought, and then I asked again, "Can you please tell me how I can reach her?"

It took a moment longer to respond but then some words appeared again: "Professor Eugenio Gambetta, Colombina Mental Asylum."

I really would have preferred a more detailed explanation but I had to take it as it was, so I said my thanks and ended our communication.

Who the devil was this Professor Eugenio Gambetta? I'd never heard of him. Was he perhaps one of those shrinks who worked at the asylum? Unfortunately I was well-acquainted with that place after having been locked up there once for a week.

It had all happened one summer a few years back, because of some experiments I'd been conducting along the city's sunny streets in which I was attempting to speak to lizards with the aid of strange device I'd invented and constructed.

Unfortunately some people are simply unable to accept anything that goes beyond their own limited little minds, which at times are narrower than a tiny broom closet!

The Colombina Mental Asylum was a terrible place – my memories of it were awful. If you weren't already crazy when you were admitted, they'd make you crazy. As soon as you were in the door, even before asking for your name, they stuffed you full of pills. This caught me by surprise. It prevented me from turning immediately into the hairy, sharp-toothed monster, Grunz, which would have resolved the situation in no time. I was able to do so only after a week, having secretly tossed my daily ration of pills out the window. In the days following my escape they'd tried to track me down but their attempts had failed, for when they'd captured me I was carrying false documents from my recent top-secret mission to the Far East.

Given these precedents, I wasn't exactly enthusiastic about having to set foot back there, but there was no other choice, so I went. We can't always do what we want to do.

Naturally I avoided going in through the main entrance so as not to be recognized, opting instead for a window at the back which someone had carelessly left open. I darted unseen through a maze of stairs and hallways until I reached the head doctor's office, where I imagined the register with the list of doctors was kept. Luckily the office was deserted and it didn't take me long to find what I was looking for. Unfortunately, however, no Professor Eugenio Gambetta worked there. I was once again beginning to have my doubt about Onofria's sphere when I glimpsed a second register. I opened it to discover that it was a list of patients, and there I found the name of the man I was looking for with the indication of the cell in which he was being held, number 117.

It was then that my luck abandoned me. The head doctor suddenly appeared, accompanied by three brawny male nurses. I was amazed at his excellent memory, for as soon as he saw me he recognized me and exclaimed, "It's that lizard guy. Quick, get him!"

Luckily the nurses had good memories too. Well did they remember my transformation into the monster Grunz and the beating they'd taken! They didn't budge. I thus set off calmly towards the door with every intention of making myself scarce, but the head doctor had a surprise in store for me. The last time, when he'd found out about my escape and particularly about my transformation, and when he remembered that a small phial of my blood remained the laboratory, that loon of a doctor of loons had injected himself with my blood in a rash attempt to acquire my preternatural power for himself. Thus he was now capable of mutating into a monster that vaguely resembled Grunz and he'd also acquired the ability to shape-shift at will.

He turned into a mangy bulldog of a monster and made his stand in front of the door, growling in an attempt to prevent me from leaving.

The poor fool thought he'd able to compete with me, but he was totally out of his league. It was one thing to have a small phial of my blood circulating in his veins; it was quite another to be the one who produces that blood. When I transformed in turn and he found himself in front of the hairy, sharp-toothed monster, Grunz, he let out a yelp and ran to take refuge under the desk with his tail between his legs.

I was almost grateful to him for having provoked my transformation since I could thus take advantage of my increased strength and speed to run up to cell number 117, tear off the door, throw Professor Eugenio Gambetta over my shoulder, and take him away with me by jumping down from a second-story window.

CHAPTER 7

I ran all the way out to the countryside and only stopped when we were in the middle of a field, far away from prying eyes. Soon after, I reverted to my usual features and as usual had to bang my head against something hard, in this case a tree, to alleviate the terrible headache that always afflicted me after my transformation.

Strangely, Professor Eugenio Gambetta didn't seem the least bit perturbed by what had transpired. Being kidnapped by an unknown monster seemed for him to be the most natural thing in the world. Indeed, as soon as I'd reassumed my normal appearance and finished banging my head against the tree, he came up to me all smiles and with hand outstretched, saying, "Many thanks for helping me escape from that horrible place. I was beginning to think I'd never get out alive."

I realized immediately that he too had ended up there not because of mental illness, but as the victim of those responsible for locking him up. "No thanks necessary," I replied, "and you really must excuse me if I was a bit brusque, but there simply wasn't time for exchanging courtesies."

"Of course, of course. Generally I'm not one for formalities either, so let's do away with them altogether. Your transformation - very interesting. It's extremely rare in this day and age to find individuals who've maintained the capabilities that belonged to all humans back before the time of Lemuria. When you banged your head against the tree, it was because of the headache, correct? Of course, of course. The cranium of modern man is too small to allow for such cerebral expansion."

Then he looked around, took a deep breath and said, satisfied, "How wonderful it is to be free again in the open air! Today is a beautiful day."

He really was quite the character, and his appearance lived up to his personality: a white moustache and goatee, sharp, lively eyes behind a pair of round spectacles, both calm and alert at the same time.

"And now would you be so kind," he continued, "as to tell why you've taken the trouble to set me free?"

I told him about the Principality of Minutia and Lorelai's mysterious disappearance.

"Nothing mysterious about it," he affirmed as soon as I'd finished. "In order to enter a parallel dimension, you most certainly have to disappear from the one you're in."

"Parallel dimension?"

"Certainly, and this is just the reason why they locked me up in the Colombina. They saw me as I was attempting to enter one of them. Some people will condemn anything they can't understand."

In truth I wasn't all that surprised by this story of parallel dimensions given that, normally, people already live closed off to one another, each in his own dimension, some of which are destined never to meet.

Professor Gambetta launched into a complicated explanation.

"There exist," he said, "innumerable dimensions: parallel, perpendicular, convergent, divergent, concentric, supersonic, polyphonic, and so on and so forth. The fundamental difference between them is the vibratory frequency of their atoms. This is why they can coexist in the same space without getting in each other's way."

Even if his explanation was quite interesting, I was on the verge of falling asleep. It was a reflex I'd been forced to develop during the incredibly tedious and interminable Entomology classes I'd attended while studying the lives of hornets at the University of Zagreb. So I decided to come right to the point and ask him, "So the Principality of Minutia is located in the exact same position as our city?"

"Yes, it has the same location of your city, but not of mine. I live somewhere else, and to tell you the truth I can't wait to get back there and put as much distance as possible between me and the Colombina Mental Asylum. I gave them a false name so they'll never be able to track me down."

It seemed this expedient was used more often that I'd thought.

"If you agree," he went on, "I'll show you how to get to Minutia and then I'll skip town. But we're going to need a few things: a pair of sunglasses, a Napoleonic bicorn hat, two sticks of sandalwood, sulfur, saltpeter, and sugar. Do you know where we can find them?"

"I think we've got it all at the house," I replied.

"Excellent, then let's get to it," he said.

CHAPTER 8

When we arrived at the house, we immediately set about searching for the things we needed. Going through the library on our way to the attic, the professor was fascinated by the great number of antique volumes it contained.

"Look here!" he exclaimed suddenly, taking from the shelf an old book covered in dust and entitled *Passages Between Dimensions*. "This is the fundamental text upon which I've based all my studies. I thought mine was the only existing copy. Therein is described everything you must do to pass from one dimension to another."

That said, he opened it and showed me a series of illustrations in which you could see a man in his underwear wearing a bicorn and sunglasses and holding two sticks ablaze at the ends while he carried out a series of complicated steps and turns, right up to the point when he disappeared in a great cloud of smoke.

I began to understand why Professor Gambetta, surprised in the act of this strange performance, had been locked up in the asylum.

What's more, I wasn't the least bit enthusiastic about having to perform this circus act myself, but if that was the only way to rescue Lorelai then I certainly wouldn't back out.

However, my lucky star once again came to my aid. I suddenly saw Professor Gambetta jump, then climb squirrel-like up the ladder to reach one of the highest shelves, and there grab a volume even older and dustier than the first.

"It's not possible, it's not possible ..." he repeated as he climbed down, blowing so much dust off the book that he nearly suffocated. Once he was back on the ground, he showed it to me and said, "It was thought this book had disappeared a thousand years ago."

I saw written on the cover: *Secret Life of the Egyptian Marmot*.

Now I've always had the greatest respect for the natural sciences and for those who practice them, but in all honesty it didn't really seem to me the most opportune moment to get so excited about a similar book.

Reading my mind exactly, Professor Gambetta hurried to explain. "Don't you get it? The Egyptian marmot doesn't exist!"

At that point I was really beginning to regret having broken him out of the asylum.

Finally he got to the heart of the matter. "This is the most important treatise ever written about passing between the various dimensions and its contents are so secret that the cover is purposely false and misleading!"

Since I didn't know whether or not to believe him anymore, I took the book from his hands and opened it.

It was all true. The title on the inside was completely different - *Key Words to Enter and Exit the 1,024 Known Dimensions*. Its author was the sorceress Onofria.

When I told the professor that I also possessed Onofria's sphere he nearly fainted.

I gave him a glass of unripe cucumber juice, of which I had extensive reserves, and with that he came to.

"All right," he said, "let's not think about the sphere for the moment but rather concentrate on the book. With this we can enter and exit any dimension at our leisure with no need for any strange rituals. For example, it seems to me that the Principality of Minutia is located in the dimension of the Seventh Dragon. Let's go see what its key words are."

He opened the heavy volume and set about searching until he found the right page.

"Here we are!" he exclaimed happily. "Dimension of the Seventh Dragon. Entrance word 'Arjxhkliop', exit word 'Poilkhxjra.' As you may have noticed, one word is the inverse of the other, but then even children know that."

Children? What children? Truth be told I hadn't noticed much of anything. It seemed to me it was already quite an accomplishment just being able to pronounce correctly a similar jumble of letters.

"How come when you pronounced them you didn't end up in the other dimension?" I asked him.

"The 'why' is explained here at the beginning," he said as he flipped the pages of the book backwards, and as he did so, I realized that on their edges was depicted a series of small images that formed a cartoon - the cartoon of a small wizard doing somersaults.

"Nice, eh?" said the professor. "Onofria could be quite the artist as well, and she amused herself by creating little games of this sort."

Finally he found the page he'd been looking for.

"Okay, here it explains that the key words must be pronounced while standing on one leg, the left." Good, at this point I knew all there was to know. So I pocketed the little piece of paper with the key word that would allow me to get back, put on my jacket with reinforced elbows, and packed underneath it my trusty carbon-reinforced, double oblong-barreled, k16 Fergusson pistol. I thanked and said good-bye to Professor Gambetta, telling him that if he wanted to wait for me there he could make himself at home, but that if he wanted to go he should leave his address so I could pay him a visit. Then I pronounced out loud and on one leg the word 'Arjxhkliop' and disappeared into thin air like a ghost at the first light of dawn.

A moment later I was already back, half burned to a crisp.

"Do you mind telling me just where in the devil you sent me? A circle of hell, perhaps? There were flames everywhere and dragons flying around all over."

"Really? Gosh, then I must have made a mistake."

He thought it over a moment and then exclaimed, "Of course! How stupid! The dimension of the Seventh Dragon is the one with the war of fire! The Principality of Minutia, rather, should be in the dimension of the Twelve Volcanoes."

"The Twelve Volcanoes, eh? Listen, don't take this the wrong way, but I think I'm going to go ask for confirmation from Onofria's sphere," and with that I returned to the library, followed by the professor.

CHAPTER 9

The sphere did not confirm the information proffered by Professor Gambetta, who was forced to admit that he really wasn't much of an expert on dimensional names. On the other hand, there were so many of them that knowing them all was nearly impossible. We thus discovered that the Principality of Minutia was not located in the dimension of the Twelve Volcanoes, but rather in that of the Yellow Stone. I put the paper with the correct key words in my pocket and once again said good-bye to the professor. This time, however, he barely answered because his attention was fixed on by the sphere, to which he was posing an infinite series of questions of a more or less scientific nature. As I disappeared for the second time, I heard him asking how high a female flea could jump. It was a query devoid of any interest for me, but no two of us are completely alike, are we? I thought that in all likelihood I'd find him still there asking questions upon my return.

An instant later I made my entrance into the new dimension, where I found a far less hostile environment than the one in which I'd ended up before. Truth be told, the place was completely familiar in that it was exactly the same one from which I'd departed, that is, the library of my own home. Yet the great bookshelves bursting with volumes had vanished and in their place were gym machines of various types, punching bags, wall bars, poles, ropes and so forth. It seemed in every way to be a gym, yet there was something sinister in the air. Everything was run-down, the ground was dirty, and some of the ropes that hung from the ceiling ended in a noose. Leaning against the walls were wooden likenesses of the same man, pompously dressed, fat and sneering, pierced by knives and arrows. It was strange to find myself in an environment that was at the same time both so familiar and so alien. All of a sudden I felt a chill run down my spine. It was bizarre because, despite everything, I wasn't in the least bit afraid, but everything was suddenly clear when I saw Death appear in front of me with a chessboard in tow.

"It's useless changing dimensions," he told me. "There is no place I cannot find you."

It was obvious he was not acquainted with the anti-everything bunker constructed by my great-great-grandfather Theobald in collaboration with the wizard Crispin of Cornwall. I'm not completely sure, but I truly think that if I hid out down there, not even he would be able to find me quite so easily.

Even though it still did not seem to be the most opportune moment to sit down and play, this time I decided to humor him. We cast lots for colors and I got the whites, after which we arranged the pieces on the board and the game began. We decided that in this first session we'd make five moves each, so I made my five moves and came within a step of check-mate, and then sat back calmly to wait for him to make his. Yes indeed, I'd given it a shot and he'd nearly fallen for it, but after a moment of confusion he protested, "Hey, not five moves in a row, but one for each of us in turn!"

"Oh yes, you're right, sorry. I was distrac-ted. Who knows what I was thinking?"

I rearranged everything and made a move. Slightly annoyed but also amused, Death said, "Don't play stupid with me" and made his move in turn.

Nothing much usually happens during the first five moves of a game of chess, but that time I managed to lose a bishop, most likely because I wasn't concentrating enough. I con-soled myself thinking that I'd recoup in our next meeting. Death, on the other hand, see-med quite satisfied.

"Laugh now," I said to him, "since in the end you just might be crying."

This was certainly some idiotic blustering of the highest level, but I couldn't help it.

"Know that I don't laugh or cry ever," he re-plied.

I thought to myself that he certainly wasn't the expressive type.

Since I didn't feel much like conversation and really wanted to discover who in that dimension lived in my house, I politely said good-bye to him and we agreed to meet again the following day.

After he disappeared, I set off towards the door to go downstairs. I was about to open it when I heard some voices approaching, so I turned back and went to hide behind a large trunk.

I expected to see a band of thugs come in and in fact that was exactly what I saw, save for one detail. Amidst the pack of hoodlums there was beautiful young woman with long dark hair and green eyes. The strange thing is that - wouldn't you know it? - they were all wearing a jacket with reinforced elbows identical to mine.

We should never judge people by their outward appearance. This was a lesson I'd long since learned, at least from that time I'd mistaken the lead singer of the band "Dead Meat" for a bum and offered him a few cents, thus unleashing the fury of his fans. Since on that occasion it hadn't seemed wise to turn into the hairy, sharp-toothed monster, Grunz, I ran for my life and had to flee for three blocks before I was able to lose them.

Well, this time too I'd been fooled by appearances. For as I listened to their conversation from my hiding place, I realized that I wasn't dealing with a pack of brigands but with a group of revolutionary idealists who were fighting against the tyranny of a certain Grand Duke Sylvester, who happened to be the pompous potbelly whose likenesses pierced by arrows and daggers adorned the room.

Their discussion became particularly interesting when they began to speak of Lorelai.

One of them said, in fact, "Ever since General Cannon brought that usurper here, things have precipitated."

It didn't take a genius to figure out whom they were talking about.

"Soon there'll be the coronation," affirmed the black-haired girl. "We must act before it's too late."

"If the case of new crossbows doesn't arrive" argued another, "we won't be able to free Princess Giovanna."

I recognized the last speaker as the man who'd attacked us in the park as we were returning home after the concert.

I decided to delay no longer in revealing myself. I rose to my feet and said, "Don't worry, we'll find a way to make everything work out. You'll see that with a bit of courage, commitment and luck, we'll succeed in our intent." Everyone turned towards me. I was smiling but prepared for the worst. I expected them all to jump me from one moment to the next. Instead, they unexpectedly just stood there still with an amazed expression on their faces. There was a long minute of silence. You could have heard a pin drop, if anyone had dropped one. Perhaps what was stopping them was that I had a jacket identical to theirs, or a monster had appeared behind me and they were paralyzed with fear, or maybe in their dimension things sometimes stopped like this for no reason at all, as if someone had pressed 'pause.' In the end it was the girl who broke the silence.

"Are you the one who comes from another dimension?"

"Yes. How did you guess?"

She turned to her comrades and exclaimed: "The prophecy has been fulfilled! We must doubt no longer! Princess Giovanna shall be freed and shall take the throne!"

CHAPTER 10

Everyone cheered. Everyone, that is, except for that thin bald man with the long, thin black moustache who had attacked us in the park.

"Don't trust him!" he exclaimed. "I recognize him! He was with the usurper in the other dimension! He's the one who prevented me from killing her."

Why is it that, whatever situation you happen to be in, there's always a spoilsport.

"That doesn't mean anything!" the girl fired back. "The wizard Rondella predicted that a man would arrive from another dimension to set things right and Rondella has never lied!"

"Not even that time about the chocolates?" asked the man with the thin moustache with a smirk.

"That was the exception that proves the rule," replied the black-haired girl. "Listen, even if you are our leader, your lack of faith in Rondella is really unbearable!"

Having said this, she came towards me smiling with her hand outstretched. Whether or not they're in charge, women always have the last word.

I noted with some surprise that her hair which had previously been black was now suddenly copper-colored. I later found out that in this dimension, women could change their hair color at will, much to the disappointment, I would imagine, of local hairdressers. Having a trick like that up her sleeve would not have displeased Lorelai in the least.

"Welcome to the secret hideout of the Giovannists," she said to me. "My name's Babette."

"A pleasure to meet you," I replied as I shook her slender hand.

So it was that I discovered that my house in that dimension was none other than a cove of revolutionaries, loyal whether rightly or wrongly to this Princess Giovanna. In any case our aims appeared to coincide since neither I nor they wanted Lorelai to take the throne.

I wanted to know a little more about them though so I asked Babette, "Who is this Princess Giovanna?"

"There! I knew it!" exclaimed the man with the thin black moustache. "This guy doesn't know anything about anything and we're supposed to entrust ourselves to him!"

"Now that's enough!" I silenced him. "Haven't you heard what the prophecy says? I am the chosen one. So now please keep quiet."

I then whispered to Babette, "Is he really your leader? He doesn't seem very in tune with the rest of the group."

"He's the one who started our movement, but he's never believed in Rondella's prophecy, to which the rest of us are staunchly dedicated. This aside though, he's all right. You can trust him blindly."

"What's his name?"

"Judas."

Judas? Right there and then I was a bit perplexed, but then I considered that in that dimension they had certainly had a different history than ours and thus the personages from our past didn't necessarily coincide with theirs. I'd certainly never trust him with my house keys, though.

"Come," Babette said to me, "let's go to the green room so we can sit down at the table and talk for a bit." Once on the ground floor I turned without hesitation towards the green room as I knew very well where it was. Everyone was amazed and, as usual, Judas took advantage of the situation to try to discredit me. "Just how did you know where the green room was? I'll bet you didn't come from another dimension at all and that you're a spy of the grand duke instead." At that point I lost what was left of my patience, grabbed him by the collar and, looking him straight in the eyes, asked him, "Listen, just who are you? Judas or Saint Thomas? You don't believe in anything, do you?" To convince him that I came from another world I thrust in his face my membership card from the Indifference Club, whose members set out to achieve total ataraxy.

Naturally, my reference to Saint Thomas was lost on them but the membership card to my club had the desired effect since nothing like it existed in their dimension.

While we sat around the table, four of them began to serve drinks. They went down to the cellar and returned soon after laden with bottles that were quickly uncorked. They all began to drink heavily while I limited myself to a small taste. The reason why the Giovannist movement had still not amounted to anything and why they hoped for outside assistance was now immediately clear to me. After about fifteen minutes they were all completely drunk. Even Judas was showing clear signs of inebriation, though in truth I hadn't seen him drink as much as the rest of them. It wouldn't be the first time in history that one side in a conflict had defeated itself. I had a classic example right before my eyes.

Even so I had been able to find out something useful: that the Giovannists – when they were sober – were fighting against the hated Grand Duke Sylvester, who'd been named Regent after the much-loved Prince Manolete Speneloto had died of indigestion. The latter's only daughter, Princess Giovanna, was in fact still too young to inherit the throne. Despite the fact that the principality was quite rich, the grand duke starved his people and didn't want the legitimate heir to take the throne since she would have immediately stripped him of power and had him arrested. He had therefore had her confined to a wing of the palace where he'd kept her prisoner for years. Now that Giovanna was about to reach her majority and the grand duke would have to relinquish the throne to her, he'd set about looking for another young woman of more malleable character to put in her place. In fact, since no one remembered what Giovanna looked like anymore, it would be easy for him to pass off the substitute as the real princess. However, none of the girls in Minutia would ever lend themselves to his dirty game, so the only solution was to find her elsewhere. But he didn't know where. Then one day the wizard Rondella had discovered that during a storm a bolt of lightning had opened a passage between our two dimensions. When Grand Duke Sylvester had found out, he'd immediately sent General Cannon to collect the unwitting Lorelai. This was more or less what I'd been able to find out before their conversations became too confused and incoherent due to alcohol.

Beside the grand duke's obvious miscalculation in thinking Lorelai was a girl of malleable character, there was something strange in this whole matter. There were in fact many questions that remained unanswered. How had Grand Duke Sylvester been able to organize the unripe cucumber juice point collection contest that Lorelai had won in such a short time?

How could he have been so sure that a young woman would have won it, and not some fat fishmonger? Why was Judas, despite having drunk very little, pretending to be just as drunk as the others? What kind of a name was Manolete Speneloto? Would it rain tomorrow or would it be sunny? Had I remembered to pay the last installment of my club's membership dues?

As I asked myself these questions, the grand duke's soldiers burst into the room and arrested everyone, myself included.

CHAPTER 11

Soldiers are not generally the most delicate of people and they don't tend to tend to look too closely for subtle distinctions. For them in fact it was of little or no importance that I was neither drunk nor a Giovannist, though at that point I could certainly be considered a sympathizer. The fact that I was there and that I was wearing a jacket exactly like the others was enough to convince them I was part of the plot, a deduction that was certainly not far from the truth.

I realized with more than a little disappointment that in that dimension it was impossible for me to turn into the hairy, sharp-toothed monster, Grunz, which would have removed this unpleasant obstacle in the blink of an eye. So, as often happens in life, I was forced to bow my head and submit to an apparently adverse destiny. I could have used my trusty carbon-reinforced, double oblong-barreled, Fergusson k16 pistol that I had hidden under my jacket, but I wanted to conceal the knowledge of my technological superiority for a time when

I'd really need it. I say 'technological superiority' because I couldn't help but notice that both my friends and the guards were equipped with rather dated weapons, all of them 'manual' without exception. There was in fact an abundance of spears, swords, bows, arrows and crossbows, but nothing from which you might infer that the inhabitants of Minutia had any knowledge of firearms.

We were lined up and pushed out of the house. Considering that my drunken companions were struggling just to stay on their feet, the soldiers had their work cut out for them trying to keep an orderly line. Eventually, with the poking and prodding of their spears and swords, they were able to get the procession moving, a procession that included me.

A new surprise awaited me outside the house. In my own dimension, the house was located in the city close to a park. Here it lay in the countryside, in an isolated position outside the walls. But what most struck me was that all the rocks and stones strewn throughout the countryside were quite different than usual, for they glowed in the sun and gave off a shining, golden light. I picked a rock off the ground and saw that it was a gold nugget. No doubt about it – everywhere there was gold in great abundance and of a very high grade of purity. I could state this with certainty because I was an expert in the blond metal, having in a past life been court goldsmith to King Louis XVI, a guy who certainly didn't lack for things that sparkled. To think that once – and this is something that no one knows – he had me make him a pair of golden breeches in the vane hope of winning the heart of Henriette, one of the queen's young ladies in waiting. That girl sure made him lose his head! The funny thing is that in the end he really did lose his head, at the outset of the revolution. Fortunately I escaped just ahead of the fury of the populace, which in such cases doesn't tend to be very delicate and fails to look too closely for subtle distinctions, as we said earlier about the soldiers. I took those golden breeches and sought refuge in England where a band by the name of the Beatles was enjoying great success in those years. But it occurs to me that I might be getting a bit confused and superimposing two of my past lives, so better to end this digression and get back to our story.

Just as King Louis had hoped in vain to win over Henriette with that pair of golden breeches, I too had hoped in vain that the guards would bring us to the grand duke's palace where I might see Lorelai and let her know I was there.

But we never saw the inside of the walls. Instead we were loaded onto wagons and transported even further away from the city, directly to the stone mines.

Whenever I forgot about being in another dimension, there was always some detail there to remind me. This time it fell to the animals that were pulling our wagons. They were half-ox, half-horse and were in fact called 'horxen.' They were strong, beautiful animals and it didn't take them long to bring us to our destination.

Thus began our long days of imprisonment. During this time we poor Giovannists had no time to be bored since we were busy from morning breaking up huge masses of stone to fill Grand Duke Sylvester's treasury. Yes, that's right. Because gold was so plentiful in this bizarre dimension it was worthless while stone - humble, gray, miserable stone - was of enormous value and people were at each other's throats, so to speak, to get their hands on it.

My comrades explained to me that the stones we were breaking into rather large pieces would subsequently be worked and reduced to the size of little disks with a turkey's head engraved on one side and a cauliflower on the other - a rather questionable choice of images. They were to all intents and purposes coins, gray stone coins with a cauliflower and a turkey's head depicted on them. When I first found out about this I nearly died laughing as I thought about the idiocy of the whole operation, but then, when I'd had more time to think about it, I realized that we too did much the same in our world. Our coins of value were made of gold and had the head of some bearded personage engraved on them, but in the

A Strange Dimension

end the difference wasn't all that great. The material was different, the head was different, but the idiocy was ultimately the same.

This wasn't the first time I'd experienced a period of detention and it wasn't even one of the worst, thanks in large part to the two guards who were watching over us. Compared to that perfidious jailor who'd made my life hell during those three years I'd unjustly spent in a Cayenne prison, these two were practically angels. Physically they resembled Stan and Ollie and, as much as their position allowed, they were quite friendly to us. We all thought that they must have had no great love for Grand Duke Sylvester either. I'm not saying that sitting there breaking rocks was like being on vacation, but the situation did have some positive sides. To begin with, my comrades quit drinking. All that physical exercise kept us fit and stronger than ever and what's more, at night when we'd finished working, we spent some wonderful evenings playing the guitar and singing songs under the stars that vaguely recalled the spirituals of the American slaves. In the end, the situation we found ourselves in wasn't all that different from what theirs had been. During those evenings in the open air I also discovered that in that dimension you could see two moons instead of one in the night sky, twin moons that with each passing day waxed and waned at the same rate. A truly unique spectacle.

When at last we fell asleep, won over by exhaustion, we slept long and well.

But I always went to sleep a half-hour after the others because Death never forgot to pay me a visit. Our game continued. The fatigue of a day spent splitting stones certainly didn't help my concentration and indeed things on the chessboard weren't going too well for me. The poor whites, bereft at this point of two bishops, a castle and nearly all the pawns, struggled in stern defense of their sovereign and only rarely managed to make any forward progress, which for that matter was nearly always of little use.

CHAPTER 12

Yet there was a doubt that plagued nearly everyone, a question to which we were unable to respond: how had Grand Duke Sylvester managed to find the Giovannists' hideout, given that their plans were all still on paper and none of them had done anything to raise suspicion? Their progress up to this point didn't go much beyond launching arrows and daggers against wooden renderings of the grand duke and getting drunk on a nightly basis as they waited for some imaginary savior to arrive from another dimension.

It was thus a broadly-shared opinion that somebody had ratted them out. Who could it have been? Everyone was wondering, but I knew. For why was it that while we ate potatoes and cabbage for lunch and dinner, Judas was served exquisite delicacies, fruit and sweets? While we slept on uncomfortable mats, why was it that Judas had a foam mattress, clean sheets, and a nice pillow? And why was it that while we split rocks for twelve hours a day, Judas had been assigned the job of sitting under a tree and counting the passing swallows?

The truth seemed clear as day to me but every time I tried to explain it to the others, I was told that it wasn't possible and that Judas was above suspicion. According to them it was of no importance that their leader was Grand Duke Sylvester's cousin and had three hundred-thousand stone coins in his bank account. Ultimately, as they put it, he'd been the one who'd created their group, who'd proposed to kill Lorelai, and who'd come into my dimension to do so. Some merit indeed! Strangely however, he'd failed to carry out his mission which he could have done quite easily if he'd attacked us from behind without making that whole speech. It was my opinion that he'd only come to see if Lorelai could be the right person to take Princess Giovanna's place.

How could they be so blind? In gulping down all that alcohol, had they swallowed their brains as well?

One day I saw a small piece of paper fall from Judas' pocket. I picked it up and discovered that it was a six month-old receipt from a laundromat two streets away from my house. In my dimension! I knew that laundromat well because I'd once taken a red sweatshirt there to be washed and they'd given it back to me green, just one of the many mysteries that was scattered through my life.

That receipt was proof that Judas as well as his cousin the grand duke belonged not to this world but to mine, and that they could pass from one dimension to another long before the passage discovered by Rondella had opened up. Being quite the whiz in logical deductions, it was immediately clear to me what had happened. The inhabitants of Minutia were fundamentally good and simple folk who had lived peacefully and without problems until these two morons had come along, imprisoned their princess, and usurped power. I call them morons because instead of just grabbing all that gold which was just lying around for the taking, they'd excogitated an intricate plan to gain control of the Principality of Minutia. Their plan included both the trick of the contest with prizes to find a girl to take the place of Princess Giovanna and the unlikely plot of the Giovannists which they themselves orchestrated, and whose only objective was to arrest the conspirators and thus obtain free labor for the stone mines. They were the ones who'd introduced these naïve 'conspirators' to alcohol in order to make them even more docile, just as the colonizers of America had given firewater to the Indians in order to dull their minds and take their land.

Good, I'd figured it all out. Now all that remained was to take action. I'd have done so quite willingly if, like the rest of my comrades, I hadn't had that heavy iron ball chained to my ankle. The only solution was to attack the guards, but none of us liked that idea as we had grown quite fond of them.

One evening while singing our pseudo-spirituals under the moonlight, we saw a beautiful carriage drawn by four white 'horxen' emerge from the darkness. It came most likely from the grand duke's court and presented us with a great chance for a surprise attack. The plan was to attack the passenger as soon as he came within range and take him hostage. All of our brazen conjectures dissolved into nothing, however, when we saw climb down from the carriage none other than her, the one, the only, the incomparable Lorelai.

She was bejeweled and dressed like a princess in a long blue dress. She was gorgeous.

As soon as she saw me she exclaimed: "My little gold nugget, is that really you?"

Being called 'little gold nugget' in front of all my revolutionary comrades wasn't exactly tops in my book, but I was so glad to see her again that I barely noticed. I motioned to the others to be still and started in her direction to embrace her, completely forgetting about the ball and chain attached to my foot. I thus ended up biting the dust, face-down on the ground. This latest humiliation, added to the previous indignity of 'my little gold nugget,' was a further blow to my standing among the Giovannists, which in truth had fallen significantly since our recent mass arrest. Some had even begun to doubt whether I really was the savior of Rondella's prophecy. Luckily many of them still believed, however, thanks in large part to Babette, who was now blond and quite smitten with me.

In any case, my companions were also thrilled at Lorelai's coming since they no longer bore her any ill will after I'd told them how she'd been taken in by the contest and had absolutely no intention of usurping anything at all.

Nonetheless I heard someone yell, "It's her! It's the usurper!"

It was old Judas again, trying to strengthen his own tarnished reputation after my recent attempts to unmask him.

CHAPTER 13

Lorelai flew into my arms and told me, "It had to be you, that warrior who I'd heard had arrived from another dimension to lead the revolt against the grand duke."

After looking around she asked, "How come you let yourselves be arrested?"

I knew that behind that question there lay another, and that being: "How come you didn't turn into the hairy, sharp-toothed monster, Grunz?"

Lorelai loved this ability of mine which had so often gotten us out of trouble.

"It doesn't work in this dimension," I explained quietly, and then asked her, "And what about you? How are things going at court?"

"Just great, sweetie pie. If you only knew, all the beautiful clothes and jewels! And they all worship me and treat me like a princess. It's really quite tempting to have myself crowned for real and stay here."

A grumble of disapproval arose from the ranks of my comrades who were listening in on our conversation. Lorelai hurried to reassure them. "Oh come on, what are you thinking? I was only kidding. I know about everything. Everything! I know that Grand Duke Sylvester is a crook and that Princess Giovanna is a prisoner in the palace. My lady-in-waiting Mariangela told me, and I had her immediately arrested."

There arose an even louder grumble than before.

"Oh come on, what are you thinking?" Lorelai rushed to explain. "I had her arrested but made sure she was put with Princess Giovanna to keep her company until we came to free her. Because we are going to free her, isn't that right, my chained-up little sugar plum?"

I really wished she'd be more careful with her words, but knowing her I knew it was asking too much.

"I don't know if you know," she added, "but the coronation is planned for tomorrow evening. I came here especially to warn you."

"Tomorrow evening?!" I exclaimed. "Damn, Lorelai, why didn't you contact us earlier?"

"You can say 'damn' as much as you like if you really want to, but I only found out about you guys this morning. And I couldn't come earlier in the day because I've been busy choosing gowns, jewels, perfumes, and even dessert for the reception. I have to say it was a lot of fun."

A third grumble reached us from the Giovannists.

"Enough, already!" yelled Lorelai. "Can't you do anything besides grumbling? You should know that I've done what I've done because I was forced to. It wasn't as if I could say no! At court I'm under constant surveillance and no less of a prisoner than all of you. This evening in fact, I was only able to come here by pretending to go to sleep and then lowering myself out of a window. And anyway, wasn't it *you* who were supposed to rescue *me*? Not the opposite."

"You've come to free us?" I asked her.

"Of course! No use waiting for you ..." And that said, she presented a letter to both "Stan" and "Ollie", our two guards. As soon as they'd read them, they hurried to unshackle us. We were finally free again!

"How were you able to get these orders to free us?" I asked Lorelai as I massaged my aching ankles.

"Those aren't orders to free you, lemon pie, but letters written by the guards' wives. They say that if they don't free you right away, they'll have to deal with them."

Great feminine wisdom! I saw in this astute move all of Lorelai's subtle intelligence, and at the same time I realized how much men are conditioned by the fairer sex, sometimes inappropriately called the weaker sex.

Now that their loyalty had been compromised and their sympathy to us exposed, Stan and Ollie decided to support us wholeheartedly, assuring us that they'd be able to bring all the other soldiers in Minutia over to our revolt. Incredibly, in no time the situation had been completely turned on its head and the credit for that was all Lorelai's. Who knows, maybe Rondella was thinking of *her* when he'd predicted the arrival of a savior from another dimension?

We decided that the best moment to act would be the following evening during the coronation ceremony and Lorelai was happy as a clam, because she had one more day to live like a princess.

The plan went like this: the coronation was set for eight o'clock, so at seven we would take the bus (in reality a large, horxen-pulled wagon that offered passenger service) from the stop that was only a short walk away. Stan and Ollie would arrive beforehand and prepare the way for us ensuring the soldiers didn't move against us. Lorelai would leave a small door open for us at the back of the palace. We would enter there to stop the ceremony, arresting the grand duke and going together to free Princess Giovanna. It was crucial to act at the very moment of the coronation as the entire populace would be on hand and could thus witness firsthand the overthrow of the tyrant and, above all, lend a hand if necessary.

Good, the plan was all set as far as Lorelai was concerned! All that was remained was to say our goodbyes and fix our meeting for the next day, but since she'd come all this way she decided to stay for a little while longer and celebrate with us. As she was arriving she'd seen us singing and playing the guitar and since for her music meant dancing, she hoped to be able to do a few steps to the sound of our notes.

But as soon as the music resumed, she changed her mind, explaining that staying was too risky and that it was better to return to the palace. She gave me a kiss and got back in the carriage, behind which our two guards positioned themselves, and rapidly disappeared, swallowed up by the dark of night.

It was only when we were alone again that we realized Judas had vanished.

CHAPTER 14

Now that they'd gotten to know her, all my Giovannist friends became great fans of Lorelai and apologized for having despised and tried to kill her.

"Don't worry about it, these things happen," I replied. "It's no big deal if someone tries to kill you."

In truth I didn't know what to respond. I was preoccupied with Judas' disappearance. I feared he'd secretly boarded Lorelai's carriage in order to hurry and warn his cousin, Grand Duke Sylvester. If he had our whole plan would be at risk.

My comrades, on the other hand, weren't the least bit worried and said that I was just being paranoid - as usual. That might be, but then where was Judas? It's all well and good to be trusting and well-disposed toward your neighbor, but that doesn't mean you should give your house keys to a burglar so that he can go check whether you've forgotten to turn off the gas. Or give a long, pointy knife to a killer so that he might cut you a slice of pie. Or give the keys to a Ferrari to a reckless driver so that he might go park it for you. Well, I think the concept is clear enough. In any case there was nothing I could do about it since they were all completely indifferent to my concerns and so happy and relaxed in their new-found freedom that they got right back to playing music and singing as if they were on a trip to the countryside. The music changed its tune as well and became much more cheerful. If Lorelai had only waited a little longer, she'd certainly have enjoyed it, but it wasn't in her character to bear something that bored or depressed her for even a few seconds.

Eventually the general gaiety infected me as well, so I quit torturing myself and joined the celebrations. We continued on until very late, comforted by the thought that starting tomorrow we'd no longer be breaking rocks. Exhaustion finally got the better of us and we all fell fast asleep. Everyone except me, of course, because just like every other night Death showed up with the chess board under his arm.

"Sorry to ruin your party," he said, "but I think tonight the game is up."

"We'll see about that," I replied. I had an ace up my sleeve and was ready to use it.

As usual the chess board positioned itself perfectly horizontal in the air between us, while the pieces rearranged themselves in exactly the same positions they'd been in last time. I was unfortunately in a quite difficult position because I was left with just my king and one knight. And to think that when I participated in the Helsinki World Championship, I reached the semifinals and only lost because my alarm clock didn't ring and I didn't show up for the match! This time however, I was playing far below my usual level, most likely because I'd been spending my days splitting rocks and also because my opponent, even if I didn't like to admit it, made me a little nervous.

Despite the fact that I was usually an extremely fair and loyal player, this time I gave into the temptation to cheat, reasoning that the end justifies the means. Even if it didn't make me win, it would at least buy some time. During the previous nights, I'd sculpted a stone to form a rook that looked exactly like those on the board. The only difference was that mine was stone, while the others were made of bone. To the naked eye, however, they were identical.

"Have you seen what a beautiful moon there is tonight?" I asked Death, and when he looked up to admire it I placed the rook on the board in a position to check his king.

That was a mistake. The ground suddenly opened up beneath my feet and I fell for kilometers and kilometers, almost to the center of the Earth. I ended up sitting in the middle of what seemed to be the great circular hall of a temple. The floor was black marble and all around me there rose high columns with great doors open between them. A host of large men, similar to orcs, came through these doors and began to sing and dance around me, encircling me in a sort of grotesque ring. Each had a large napkin tied around his neck and a knife and fork in his hands. Their song went more or less like this:

Cunning fox you are, indeed!
But now a severe penalty
you've certainly earned, it can't be denied
you're a lousy cheat, that's certified!
Now we shall eat with great hunger
this foolish fop, this swaggerer!

Finally they attacked. I shut my eyes tight in preparation for impact, but feeling nothing, I opened them again. I found myself suspended in infinite space where I could see the stars shining in the dark and the planets placidly tracing their orbits.

I heard a celestial music and a voice saying, "Do you see? Everything is in harmony."

Then suddenly I felt myself falling, and as I fell I almost lost consciousness until I found myself seated once again at my place in front of the chessboard. My stone rook had disappeared and Death was still looking at the moon.

"Yes, it's very beautiful," he said. "Now move – it's your turn."

Very well, I'd learned my lesson. I made my

move, then he made his, then me again, then him again, and that was that because he'd checkmated me.

"You didn't play poorly," said Death, as he made the chessboard vanish with a gesture of his hand, "considering everything that's happened to you in the meantime."

"It's no big deal," I replied. "Sometimes you win and sometimes you lose. I guess I won't be able to complete my mission now."

"Why is it that you mortals always have something to complete?"

"Not always. I often don't have anything to do."

"Listen, now I really must be going because I have another engagement."

"I certainly won't stop you."

"I shall be back to collect you tomorrow evening."

"Excellent, there's no rush. An extra day just might be enough for me."

Death wrapped himself up as usual in his black cloak and began to disappear but then thought better of it, came back and said, "But you should know that there's still a way for you to save yourself."

"Oh yeah?"

"Yes."

Then he was silent.

I didn't want to give him the satisfaction of seeming too interested so I asked him with the greatest possible nonchalance, "So let's hear it then, what is the way?"

"I can't tell you. You'll have to discover it for yourself."

That said, he began to disappear once again but I was just in the nick of time to add, "At least give me a clue."

"Buy two and get one" was his response, at which point he definitively vanished.

Buy two and get one? Besides being a damned cryptic answer, it didn't strike me as much of a deal either. At any rate I was too tired to think about it so off I went to bed.

CHAPTER 15

The next morning there was finally no wake-up call so we could sleep as long as we wanted. We were all so exhausted that perhaps we went a bit overboard and got up well into the afternoon. Indeed it was five o'clock when the first of us cracked an eye open and wisely decided to get everyone else out of bed as well.

Unfortunately, for breakfast there was only the usual cabbage with potatoes so we had to make do with that. Anyone who complains about having cabbage as a mid-afternoon snack has obviously never tried it for breakfast. In any case we were well-rested, if not equally well-nourished, and given that it was already almost seven o'clock, we went to catch the bus as per our plan. An unpleasant surprise was in store for us, however. We found a note hanging from the bus stop that read: "Twenty-four hour strike today. We apologize for any inconvenience this may cause."

We were dismayed. Everyone except me, that is, as I'd long since become utterly impassive.

Keeping my cool, I quickly reviewed the various possible solutions and finally exclaimed: "Quick, everybody run! There's no time to lose!"

My comrades looked at each other. They hesitated. Eventually they saw there was no other choice. So at a quick space we set off toward the city, a band of revolutionaries left stranded in the moment of truth.

How I wished I'd brought with me my seven-league boots, which were hidden somewhere in my trophy room! Even if I'd been able to go get them, however, finding them would have been no easy task given the indescribable chaos that reigned in there. Just think that the last time I'd gone in there, the great bronze statue of Ergon the Wise had collapsed right in front of the door. It was only by turning into the hairy, sharp-toothed monster, Grunz, that I'd been able to lift it up and get out of the room.

Meanwhile, as I recalled these things I continued to run alongside the others. At a certain point one of us, I can't remember who, had an idea: to save energy we'd take turns riding on each other's shoulders so that everyone would have a chance to rest. This turned out to be a really terrible idea because by so doing we all felt twice as tired and ran only half as fast. So we went back to running normally, though following our initial sprint we were now staggering along more than running, huffing and puffing like so many pistons. As usual I say 'we' but I'm referring to my friends the Giovannists, who owed this shortness of breath to their deplorable alcoholic past. I on the other hand had no problem because my legs conserved the strength they'd acquired in a past life when I'd run messages from Emperor Montezuma in the city of Tenochtitlan through the Andes to the sister cities of Texcoco and Tlatelolco.

We finally came in sight of the city of Minutia and it was just in time, as my comrades could hardly muster the energy to stand up. One of them, the usual guy, proposed we all lie down on a grassy meadow for ten minutes to catch our breath, but this time we ignored him and continued running. We thus made our entrance into the city, where we found the streets completely deserted because everyone had gone to the coronation ceremony. There weren't even any dogs. Well, I should say I wish there hadn't been any, because after a while a mongrel started running after us and barking like a lunatic. Then it was the turn of a German Shepard, then a Labrador, two more mongrels, a basset hound, a boxer ... in brief, by the time we got to the little door at the back of the palace that Lorelai had left open for us, we were being chased by two dozen dogs barking as if they were out of their minds. So much for passing unobserved!

At this point the guy who'd had the brilliant idea of running with someone on our shoulders and had then proposed lying down on the grass for a nap came up with another stroke of genius. Naturally, it never rains but it pours. He had a backpack with him whose contents were unknown to the rest of us. He opened it and we discovered it was full of cabbages, a food he adored to no end. He'd taken an ample supply away from our prison camp, and now he took them out, probably quite reluctantly. He began to throw them to the dogs to try to calm them down with what for him was a real delicacy.

The dogs did indeed stop barking for a moment, but as soon as they'd tasted the cabbage they made a strange face and then launched themselves at us. If they could have spoken they would surely have yelled: "Revenge! Revenge!"

I'd like to point out at this juncture that I don't personally have anything against cabbage, a food which I actually enjoy when I'm not forced to eat it breakfast, lunch and dinner for weeks on end. But it's easily understandable that dogs might not necessarily share these views.

Fortunately I had immediately grasped the intention of our reckless companion and anticipated the consequences of his thoughtless act. So I hastened to get everyone inside the palace through the narrow little door. I was able to slam it shut at the very last moment on the snouts of those cabbage-incited beasts.

Once inside, we set about wandering through the corridors and rooms of the palace in search of the main hall where the ceremony was being held. The trouble was that the little door was the last of the service entrances, and thus the farthest from our objective. So we first had to pass through the servants' quarters where we found some of them sound asleep, oblivious to the historic event then underway in the palace, then through the laundry rooms where we found a launderer and a launderette also indifferent to the coronation who were rolling around together among the princely sheets, and finally through the kitchens, where several waiters and waitresses took advantage of the general commotion to indulge in an abundant sampling of the refreshments that were supposed to follow the ceremony. We also passed through the room of Caesar Octavian Augustus, the grand duke's beloved dog, a gigantic Great Dane who barely looked up from the bone he was chewing on, a bone so big it could easily have belonged to a dinosaur.

As far as palace visits were concerned it was certainly very interesting, but we were wasting precious time. Eight o'clock was now well and truly behind us so I decided to ask for directions from the first soldier we met, just as people normally ask a policeman for directions in a city they're not familiar with. This would also allow me to verify whether Stan and Ollie, that is our ex-prison guards, had truly convinced the militia to come over to our side.

I was relieved to discover that our two friends had kept their word. Indeed the four soldiers we bumped into willingly escorted us to the throne room where we made our entrance, passing down the main hallway no less, between the two groups of onlookers crowded behind the barriers.

The room was immense and had been decorated for the important occasion. Floral ornamentation covered both the walls and the numerous columns that held up the extremely high ceiling, from which hung enormous and incredibly heavy stone chandeliers rich in quartz and crystals.

We arrived just in time to see the grand duke place the crown on Lorelai's head, his loyal cousin Judas at his side.

Stunned, my comrades exclaimed, "Did you see that? It's not possible! Judas is with the grand duke! Maybe he was a traitor after all!"

They'd finally awoken from their slumber.

The grand duke solemnly declared: "With this crown I pronounce you Princess of Minutia and simultaneously marry you, thus becoming your prince consort and assuming all powers possible and imaginable, admissible and inadmissible, absolute and dissolute, high and low, here and there and up and down. This I affirm in virtue of the secret code of Tricks and Tracks contained in the ninth volume of the great encyclopedic treatise of Mustafa the Headless a.k.a. the Mysterious Trumpeter. Thus I have done and thus I have said, he who says differently is a dunderhead."

CHAPTER 16

That was one of those rare times in which my imperturbability was really put to the test. I was shocked, to say the least. Never had I heard such a ridiculous speech made for such an important ceremony. Setting aside for the moment that final rhyme fit for nursery school, what was all that chatter about Tricks and Tracks, the encyclopedic treatise, the mysterious trumpeter, absolute and dissolute powers, here and there and up and down? It was the usual smoke being blown into the eyes of the people so they might bow down before things they did not understand. Poor Lorelai! If she absolutely had to get married, she could at least have done so with a bit more dignity!

Regarding the wedding as such, I wasn't the least bit concerned since rites celebrated in another dimension clearly weren't binding for us 'aliens.'

But the moment had come to act. My Giovannist friends, distraught at having arrived too late, stood there with their mouths agape. I might as well have been surrounded by a school of tongue-tied fish. Once again they showed they weren't worth much as revolutionaries.

I took a step forward and exclaimed: "Everyone freeze! Nobody move! This is a robbery!"

Why I'd said this last part was a real mystery. Maybe in a past life I'd been a gangster or something similar and it was still having an effect on me. In any case it wasn't the right thing to say, so I immediately corrected myself: "What I meant was … everyone freeze! This wedding is not to be performed, not today, not ever!"

This second effort of mine was decidedly better than the first one, though certainly not the essence of originality. At this point I expected the soldiers, converted to the revolt by our Stan and Ollie, to take action and go arrest the grand duke and his cousin and the populace to rise up close behind them, but no one lifted a finger. A silence as heavy as a boulder fell over the room. Not even the buzz of a fly could be heard. A fly did take a peak through one of the windows, but given the situation it immediately turned around. It was Lorelai who finally broke the silence.

"My late-arriving little sweetie pie!" she exclaimed. "Does this seem to you like the time to burst in?"

She took the crown off her head, returned it to the grand duke, lifted up her long dress so as not to trip, and ran toward me. At this point something truly unexpected occurred, because the grand duke who still hadn't said a word suddenly let out a roar and transformed into a monster whose appearance was peculiar to say the least. It was a mix between a gorilla, a bison, a shark and a walrus. I'd never seen anything like it, except maybe in a work by Picasso. Judas mutated as well, turning into a sort of huge crested snake with the ears of an elephant. Pretty crazy stuff! Anyway now it was all clear. The grand duke and his cousin didn't come from Earth as I'd imagined, but from another dimension entirely, probably that of Unlikely Monsters. Having somehow arrived in Minutia, they'd acquired the power to shapeshift and thus morphed to fit in with the inhabitants of this place. Until that moment their plan to take power had proceeded seamlessly, but my intrusion in the middle of the ceremony and, above all, the lack of any intervention by the soldiers had made it clear to them that things had changed. Thus they'd reassumed their true shapes to attempt one last desperate move.

Meanwhile, Lorelai had reached me and as I held her tightly in my arms I whispered to her, "Your husband's not very good-looking. Mind telling me what you saw in him?"

"Don't worry honey," she replied, "I've already asked for a divorce."

Then I yelled at the monster-grand duke and his snake-cousin: "Surrender! Your dirty game is up! Don't you see that the entire populace is ready to march against you?"

I turned around for confirmation of this but, alas, behind us now there wasn't a soul. The great hall which until a few seconds ago had been almost impossibly full of men, women and children was now completely deserted. Only Lorelai and I were left to take on the two monsters. In fact, even the soldiers had disappeared and the small group of Giovannists were huddled up in a corner of the hall with a bad case of the jitters. So as usual I had to do everything by myself, just like that time I had had to restore piece by piece the great mosaic of the Imperial Porte in the Church of Santa Sophia in Istanbul after Lorelai had brought it crashing down with a shriek provoked by a small mouse that had run between her feet. The Turkish guards immediately arrested us and the judges wouldn't listen to reason. They decided to lock Lorelai up in prison and hold her until I'd finished the restoration. I began right way and applied myself with the greatest possible effort to finish as quickly as possible but I soon realized it would take me years. So one evening I turned into the hairy, sharp-toothed monster, Grunz, and finished the job that very night. The next morning, however, the judges who'd come to examine the mosaic claimed that the composition had changed, that it wasn't the same as before, since previously there hadn't been any steam-powered locomotive, much less those penguins seated at the bar. There I lost my patience once and for all, turned back into the monster Grunz, and threw them all out the window, after which I ran to the prison, freed Lorelai, and ran all the way home carrying her on my shoulders.

Those were the days indeed when I could solve my problems so simply! Now on the other hand, this stupid dimension in which we'd ended up allowed the grand duke and Judas, that is the bad guys, to mutate at their leisure but prevented me, the good guy, from doing the same. But I still had an ace up my sleeve and I decided that the moment had come to use it. I pulled out the trusty carbon-reinforced, double oblong-barreled Fergusson k16 pistol from under my jacket and pointed it at the two monsters that had already begun to advance slowly but surely toward us. Contrary to what I'd expected, though, they weren't in the least bit impressed nor did they halt their advance. I concluded that, like the inhabitants of Minutia, they'd probably never seen a firearm before. So I decided to hold a practical demonstration by firing a shot over their heads. The explosion produced the desired effect, immediately stopping them in their tracks, but fate would have it that the bullet hit the suspension cable of one the enormous chandeliers hanging from the hall's tall ceiling, slicing it clean through. The heavy chandelier crashed to the floor precisely on the heads of the two monsters, killing them immediately.

CHAPTER 17

Lorelai and I stared as their coal-black souls left their bodies and rose up through the air, as the last puffs of smoke rise from two fires just extinguished. It was later explained to us that this was a completely normal phenomenon in that dimension and that their souls were so dark because they'd both been guilty of particularly bad conduct.

"My little *pistolero*," Lorelai said to me, "you got 'em."

"I didn't mean to," I replied as I put away my trusty carbon-reinforced, oblong double-barreled, Fergusson k16 pistol, "although you certainly can't say they'll be missed."

"You don't have to justify yourself, sugar plum, you didn't do it on purpose. And after all they certainly had it coming."

Lorelai made to give me a kiss but all of a sudden she froze, completely immobilized as if in the still frame of a film, her warm, lipstick-covered lips puckered heart-shaped and reaching out to me. I realized then that everything else around me had also frozen as if time had suddenly stood still. My Giovannist friends were frozen as they glanced at us from the corner where they'd taken refuge, the soldiers and populace were frozen as they were just beginning to re-enter through the side doors, and even a cat that happened to be passing through the back part of the hall and a butterfly that was mindlessly fluttering around the floral decorations attached to the walls were frozen.

I immediately grasped who was behind all this and in fact, a moment later he appeared. Astride a skeletal steed, wrapped up in his dark cloak and with sickle in hand, Death rose up in front of me. Looking me over from head to toe he began to speak, but I beat him to it.

"There's no need to say anything," I told him. "Let me give Lorelai one last kiss since she's already well-positioned, and then I'll come with you."

"Are you ready?"

"Are you asking if I've packed? I haven't. But if I need a toothbrush I'll just have to buy one when I get there."

"There where?" he asked curiously. "Just where the devil do you think you're going?"

"I have no idea, but there's got to be some place where you can buy the essentials."

"My friend," he responded, "you don't need anything because you're not going anywhere. Our appointment has been postponed indefinitely. I've only come to say goodbye."

"Great," I replied, "then all the best to you

as well before you change your mind. Goodbye and a pleasure to have met you."

"Know that I did not change my mind; rather it was you who did what I suggested."

"And that is?"

"Do you remember when I told you that there was still a way for you to save yourself?"

"Yes, of course. You said 'Buy two and get one.'"

"Exactly, two lives in exchange for one."

Death then spurred on his horse which proceeded to rise up on two legs and shoot away at a gallop, ascending to disappear into thin air. Truth be told, I was now even less remorseful that those two had gotten their just desserts, especially since in the end I'd been merely the blameless instrument of their punishment or, put another way, merely the last wall against which their ball had caromed.

Everything around me was suddenly reanimated and all that was left for me to do was to kiss Lorelai. It was a particularly intense kiss because for me it was the first kiss of an unanticipated new life and Lorelai couldn't help but notice.

"My fiery little sweetie pie, that was some kiss you gave me! But now's really not the time. Don't you see all the people around?"

Indeed, as often happens when you succeed in something, I suddenly found myself surrounded by a great crowd of people who were shaking my hand, declaring themselves to be my true friends, assuring me that they'd always believed I could do it, that I was the best, and that I could absolutely count on them in the future if I ever needed anything at all. Apparently they'd already forgotten that every last one of them had vanished in my hour of need. Still, I willingly accepted their displays of affection though I knew quite well that they would all disappear once more if good fortune ever deserted me again. Even General Cannon came forward, the very man, that is, who'd kidnapped Lorelai and set all these events in motion.

"No hard feelings, my boy," he said, offering me one hand to shake while with the other he smoothed out one end of his long gray moustache. "I hope you understand that I was just following orders. Deep down I truly hoped things would work out this way."

I didn't refuse his hand, but for some reason a bit of the monster Grunz's energy flowed into my hand and made me grip his hand just a little too tightly, such that the poor guy had to go right away to ice it down. The only people for whom I'd developed a real affection in all this were my old Giovannist comrades, whose late forfeit I willingly forgave them. I'd long since concluded that as combatants they weren't very reliable.

Just as we were beginning to celebrate with hugs, pats on the back and other such things, Princess Giovanna entered the hall, newly freed from her long imprisonment and escorted by a dozen soldiers.

She was quite different from how I'd imagined her, and very different from Lorelai who was, after all, the candidate to take her place. She was a gigantic woman, fat and red-faced. She didn't seem to have suffered in the least during her period of detention. She had long braids that were blond at the moment (indeed I hadn't forgotten that here women could change their hair color at will) and wore a rich, garish dress. She looked like an oversized Russian doll. I expected to see her break in half from one moment to the next and see a smaller woman emerge from within.

"Dearest," she said, smiling and extending her hands us, "let me embrace you. I know how much you've been through and I'm extremely grateful to you for all that you've done for me and my people."

She hugged us in turn and her grasp brought to mind the period in which I'd done some Greco-Roman wrestling. Lorelai barely survived her clutches and luckily I was able to stop her just in time, before she reacted by giving the princess a nice jab to the stomach. How many times had I told her not to be so impulsive!

CHAPTER 18

There was a banquet that evening and we had the honor of sitting next to Princess Giovanna. This did have its negative side, however, since the mastodon-like maiden's appetite was no less than gargantuan and she intercepted and rapidly emptied any plate which came into our vicinity, leaving us with only a few crumbs.

In this case Lorelai's audacity really came in handy, for at a certain point she 'accidentally' spilled a pot full of lentils onto the princess and thus forced her to go change her outfit. In that quarter of an hour in which the princess was gone we too were able to eat something.

Giovanna the Great, or so we jokingly called her amongst ourselves while taking care not to be overheard, insisted we stay the night in the palace and we willingly accepted. We were provided with a magnificent bedroom at the top of a tower. It was furnished in the oriental style with carpets, blankets and curtains which ranged from white to azure, turquoise, blue, and violet. That night we discovered another pleasant peculiarity of that dimension parallel to our own: when a man and woman slept together they would find themselves floating suspended in the air. It was certainly a very enjoyable and fascinating sensation, even if you had to be careful of the air currents so as not to find yourself floating right out of the window.

The next morning we woke up quite late and when we came down we found another surprise waiting for us. The previous night Princess Giovanna had hastily had a sculpture carved in my honor to acknowledge the savior of the Principality of Minutia. The statue had already been erected in the middle of the main square and everyone was waiting for us to inaugurate it.

As we went toward the site of the ceremony Lorelai whispered to me, "How wonderful, sweetie pie, I'm proud of you. Too bad we don't have a camera with us."

Upon reaching the square, after the usual trumpet blasts and drum rolls the drape covering the statue fell away to reveal my image sculpted in stone, a quite precious material in those parts. I was certainly honored by the honor accorded me, though I couldn't understand why the artist had portrayed me inside a bathtub as I scrubbed my back with a long brush.

I asked for clarification and the princess explained to me that the sculptor had intended to symbolize both my pure and immaculate spirit and the return of the Principality of Minutia to a period of candor and clarity after so much filth.

Pretty crazy stuff. Lorelai simply repeated what she'd already said before, that being, "Too bad we don't have a camera with us", but this time I suspected she said it with more than a hint of sarcasm.

"Don't think that I don't know," the princess told me, "that you would have preferred to see yourself portrayed in shining armor and perhaps atop some noble steed, but I simply couldn't interfere with the sculptor's creative energy. You see, the reason the people loved my father the prince so much is that he left everyone completely free to do as they wished and I intend to be just like him. My dynasty has been on the throne for generations because in governing it has always adopted three simple rules: few laws, few taxes, and the utmost freedom for everyone, with all due respect of course."

Well, I'll be tarred and feathered! Here was Princess Giovanna showing herself to be a truly great sovereign, and not just physically. I was about to tell her that I fully approved of her policies but Lorelai beat me to it.

"Wise words!" she exclaimed. "I totally agree with you! Freedom is the most important thing for me too, so let me shake your hand and apologize for having almost punched you in the stomach the first time we met."

"Is that so?"

I thought the moment had come to conclude this conversation so I said, "Dearest princess, unfortunately the moment has come to say good-bye because we really have to be going."

I shook her hand, made the gesture of removing my hat even if I wasn't wearing one, and finally bowed deeply while with my elbow I invited Lorelai to do likewise.

The princess however objected. "Excuse me, but just where are you planning to go? The bridge between our dimensions closed up three days ago. I fear that from now on you shall have to remain here."

"You mean the wizard Rondella's passage?" I asked, and was about to add that we didn't need it, but she didn't give me the time and replied, "Yes, that which I imagine the grand duke and his cousin used to enter your dimension in search of a puppet-princess to put in my place."

It was an incorrect supposition but not the biggest mistake she'd made. Lorelai exclaimed, her eyes wide-open, "Who are you calling 'puppet-princess'?!" and this time I wasn't quick enough to stop that jab to the stomach left over from the previous evening.

The soldiers hurled themselves at Lorelai to arrest her but Princess Giovanna stopped them.

"Let her be, it's my fault. I shouldn't have used that term," and then, massaging her stomach which had at any rate dealt quite well with the blow, added, "Well, we certainly are sensitive, aren't we?"

"I'm so sorry, princess," said Lorelai contrite-ly. "Sometimes I act without thinking. Doing so is often quite useful to me but in some cases it would better to do the contrary."

I suddenly recalled the time we were dining with Sultan Grambèl Salàm and Lorelai threw a cake in his face because she'd had the impres-sion he'd touched her backside. We risked our heads there and it was one of the innumerable occasions in which the timely intervention of the hairy, sharp-toothed monster, Grunz, had saved the day.

Lorelai however had no knowledge of either the little piece of paper or key word so she be-gan to despair. "We're going to have to stay here?! Hell's bells! I just bought my member-ship to play tennis with my friend Alexandra! And I'm signed up for a ju-jitsu course! And I have to water the flowers! And finish my carpet on the loom! And attend a series of talks about the cultivation of the silk worm! And what about my yoga lessons? And my ceramics class?"

Well, you certainly couldn't say Lorelai didn't know how to pass the time.

CHAPTER 19

"Calm down," I said to her, "the situation is under control. In my pocket is the return ticket that will take us straight home." Then I turned to Princess Giovanna and said to her with another bow: "Dearest, now we really do have to leave you. The closure of the passage is no problem for us. We're happy to have come to your aid and I hope that from now on you'll avoid getting into similar messes."

"Are you able to pass from one dimension to another at will?" asked the princess.

"For us it's as easy as drinking a glass of water."

"And you've decided to go?"

"Without a doubt, though we have enjoyed your company."

I tried to be as polite and chivalrous as possible in order to leave a fond memory of us, given that we'd probably end up in their history books.

In this same light when the princess tried to offer me compensation for what we'd done I responded magnanimously. "For me the greatest reward is to know that the Principality of Minutia is finally free and in good hands."

It was at this point that Lorelai intervened, after whispering to me, "My chivalrous little sweetie pie, you keep this up a bit longer and you'll make me nauseous," and turned to the princess, saying, "Princess Giovanna, we most willingly accept the compensation you're offering us even if we want something that has a purely symbolic value. Nothing precious then, but just a little something we can keep as a memory of this adventure of ours."

"What nobility of spirit!" the princess exclaimed. "And what could this 'little something' be?"

"A couple of sacks full of those yellow stones that pepper the countryside will be more than enough."

"You want two sacks full of ... stones?"

"Exactly. You've understood perfectly."

"But that material is of no value! It isn't even good to build with! Don't you have any in your dimension?"

"Yes we do, but we like this one more. It's more ... yellow."

"Wouldn't you prefer two sacks full of rocks from the mine?"

"Princess, please. I've already told you we don't want anything of value."

"Then it shall be as you desire!" the princess cut short, and ordered that we be given two sacks full of 'stones'.

When we were alone for a moment, Lorelai teased me. "We don't want anything, we don't want anything ... All we care about is that Minutia is free ... I guess that means that all this gold will be mine."

"All right, all right," I admitted, "I didn't think of it. You forget though that if I hadn't come to save you, by now you'd be happily married to a monster."

"Like in *Beauty and the Beast*, maybe I'd have been able to redeem him."

"I doubt it, and don't forget that I have our return ticket and, wouldn't you know, it just happens to cost a sack full of gold."

"My mistrusting little sweetie pie, there's no need for blackmail. You know I would have given it to you anyway."

"Yeah, I know. Why, do you really think I'd leave you here?"

Our conversation was interrupted by the appearance of our old friends, Stan and Ollie, pushing a wheelbarrow with two sacks full of gold inside.

"So in the end you've had your revenge," they said to me jokingly, "and made us split some rocks as well."

"Yeah, but at least yours are softer."

"But not lighter."

They left us the wheelbarrow, said goodbye and were off.

I proposed to Lorelai that we go read the key word for our return in the same spot in

which I'd arrived so as to find ourselves directly back in the library of our own house. We
thus took our leave of Princess Giovanna and
left the palace.

When we reached the house we found our
Giovannist friends wisely emptying all their re-
maining whisky bottles into the well in the
courtyard.

I don't need to point out that Lorelai was
amazed to see our house located in the open
countryside.

Once we'd climbed up to the library, we said
goodbye to everyone, we each took our sack of
gold and standing on one leg we pronounced,
in a low voice so as to conserve the secret, the
key word which in an instant brought us back
to our dear old dimension.

We looked around. We were really in the library. Lorelai put down her sack, sighed and
said: "Finally home ... and finally alone."

But a noise coming from behind us immediately contradicted her. We turned around and
saw Professor Gambetta intent on posing questions to the sorceress Onofria's sphere.

He'd been at it ever since I'd left! He was in
an awful state. Disheveled, his clothes all crea-
sed, his beard long and his eyes shadowed
with fatigue, he stubbornly continued to ask his
questions with what little voice he had left.

"Eugenio!" I exclaimed. "Don't you think
you're overdoing it just a little?"

"One more little question and then I'll stop.

One more little question and then I'll stop."

Lorelai asked me quietly, "Who is that?"

"He's a professor, of what I really don't know. I helped him escape from the asylum."

She looked at me curiously but there was no time to give her further explanations because Professor Gambetta, having gathered the last of his energy, asked the sphere, "Can you please tell me what that thing is that's there but it's not, that's everywhere but if you look for it you'll never find it, that has a thousand names and yet no name?"

At first the sphere didn't move. Then it began to vibrate faster and faster, increasing its luminosity until it became almost incandescent, until finally it all of a sudden went 'poof' and turned off.

"You broke it!" exclaimed Lorelai.

"What ridiculous questions!" I said.

"I'm mortified," babbled Professor Gambetta, "perhaps I really have overdone it."

He got up, adjusted his clothes a little, and then continued. "Now I'd better be going. I see you've got your darling back, congratulations. If the sphere doesn't work anymore you can always call me. With everything I've asked I pretty much know as much as it does."

He wrote his telephone number on a piece of paper and handed it to me, kissed Lorelai's hand, shook mine and was off with a somewhat shaky stride. As he went down the stairs he said, "Don't bother showing me out, I know the way."

We heard the front door closing so we went down as well. We sprawled out on the azure couch which was the softest of them all. I sat comfortably and Lorelai lay down, resting her little blond head on my lap. We were silent for a while and then I commented, "And to think that this all happened for those five-hundred bottle caps you sent in to that contest."

"Me?" said Lorelai. "I didn't send a darn thing. I thought that you had sent them in my name."

Then she began to hum a little tune from her native lands and went on like this for quite some time. Her silvery voice carried throughout the house.